World of Reading 1

STAR WARS™

THIS IS LUKE

WRITTEN BY NATE MILLICI
ART BY TOMATOFARM

LOS ANGELES • NEW YORK

This is Luke.
Luke lives on a
sandy planet.

But Luke is bored.
Luke wants to leave
the sandy planet.

Luke meets two droids.
The tall one is C-3PO.
The short one is R2-D2.
They have a secret message.

R2-D2 shows Luke
the secret message.
It is from Princess Leia.
She needs help.

Luke wants to help the princess.
He meets Obi-Wan.
Obi-Wan is a Jedi Knight.
He will train Luke.

Jedi Knights use the Force.
The Force is a magic energy field.
Jedi Knights use a special sword.
It is called a lightsaber.

Luke leaves the sandy planet.
He finds Princess Leia.
She is trapped on the Death Star.
Luke and Leia escape!

The Death Star is a
space station.
It can destroy planets.
Luke and R2-D2
must stop the Death Star.

Luke flies his X-wing fighter.

Luke uses the Force.

He destroys the Death Star!

Luke travels to a snowy planet.
A snow monster traps Luke.
Luke uses the Force
to reach his lightsaber.

Luke uses his lightsaber.
He stops the snow monster!

Giant AT-AT walkers stomp
across the snowy planet.
Luke uses his lightsaber to
stop them, too!

Luke goes to a swamp planet
to find Yoda.
Yoda is a Jedi Master.
Yoda is strong in the Force.

Yoda is a good teacher.
And Luke is a good student.
Yoda teaches Luke how to
be a Jedi Knight.

Princess Leia, C-3PO, and Chewie
are in trouble.
Luke leaves the swamp planet.
He must help his friends!

Luke fights Darth Vader.
Darth Vader was a great
Jedi Knight.
But he turned to the dark side.

Now Darth Vader is evil.
He wants Luke
to join the dark side.
Luke does not want
to join the dark side.

Luke faces more villains.
He escapes from
Jabba the Hutt.

He fights Boba Fett.

Luke also makes new friends.
He travels to a forest moon.
He meets the Ewoks.

Ewoks are small and furry.
They help Luke and his friends.

Luke meets Darth Vader again.
Luke is trapped!

Darth Vader takes Luke
to the evil Emperor.
He wants Luke to join
the dark side, too.

Luke fights Darth Vader
for the last time.

Luke does not give in
to fear or anger.
He will never join the dark side!

Luke is not bored anymore.
He is a brave hero.
Luke is a great Jedi Knight!

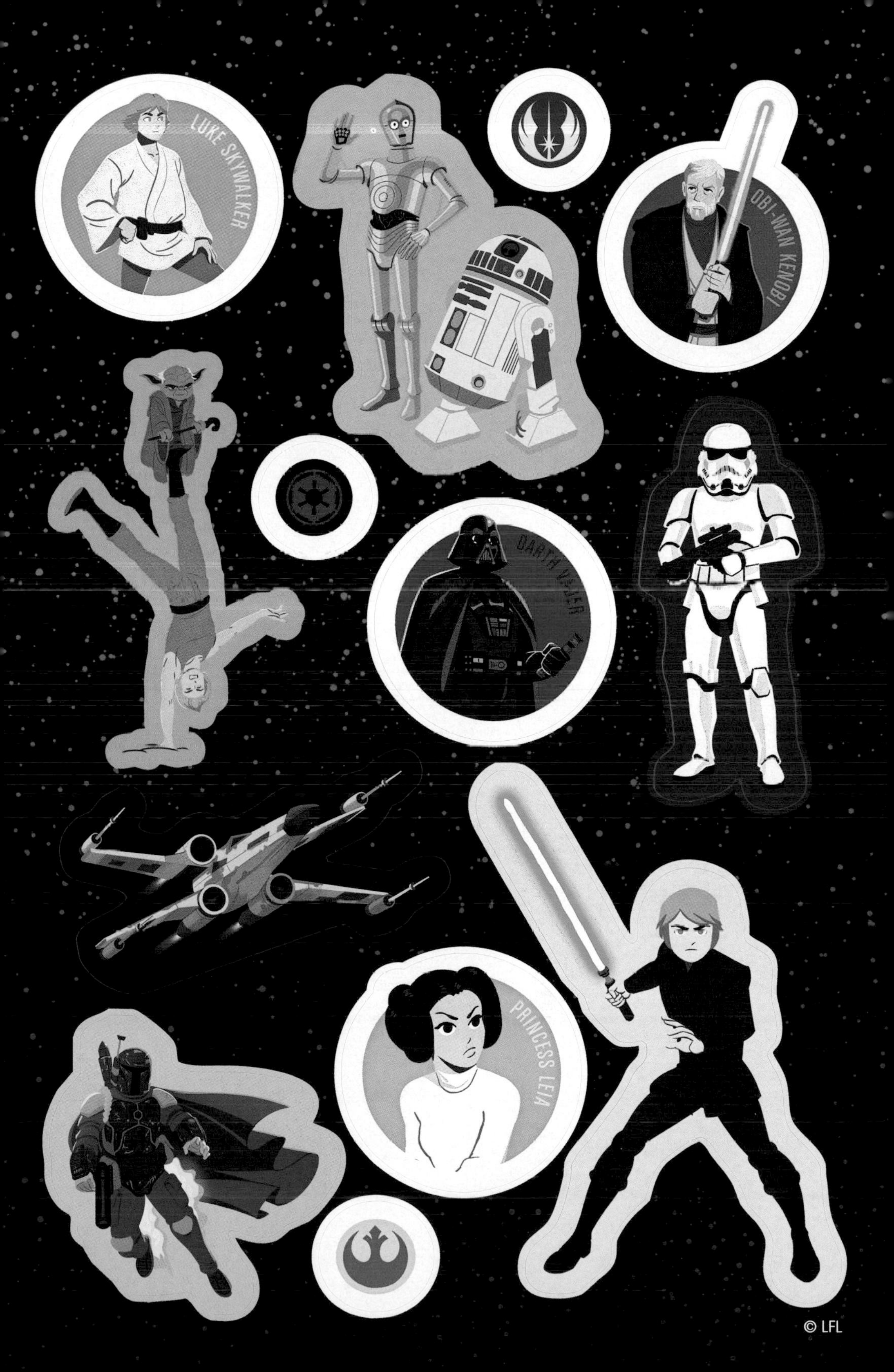
LUKE SKYWALKER
OBI-WAN KENOBI
DARTH VADER
PRINCESS LEIA